Eloise Wilkin's BABIES
A Book of Poems

Selected by Teddy Slater
Illustrated by Eloise Wilkin

A GOLDEN BOOK • NEW YORK

Western Publishing Company, Inc.

Racine, Wisconsin 53404

Acknowledgments

The editor and publisher have made every effort to trace the ownership of all copyrighted material and to secure permission from copyright holders. Any errors or omissions are inadvertent, and the publisher will be pleased to make the necessary corrections in future printings. Thanks to the following authors, publishers, and agents for permission to use the material indicated:

Aileen Fisher for "My Puppy" from *Up the Windy Hill*. Copyright © 1953 by Abelard Press, New York. Copyright renewed. Reprinted by permission of the author. All rights reserved.

Aileen Fisher for "Pussy Willows" from *In the Woods, In the Meadow, In the Sky*. Copyright © 1965 by Charles Scribner's Sons. Reprinted by permission of the author. All rights reserved.

Rose Fyleman for "The Birthday Child." Reprinted by permission of The Society of Authors as the literary representative of the Estate of Rose Fyleman. All rights reserved.

Marci Ridlon for "My Brother" from *That Was Summer*. Copyright © 1969 Follett Publishing Co. Reprinted by permission of the author. All rights reserved.

Deborah Wilkin Springett for "The Meadow" from *Eloise Wilkin's Book of Poems*. Copyright © 1988 by Deborah Wilkin Springett. Reprinted by permission of Western Publishing Company, Inc. All rights reserved.

Esther Wilkin for "A Little Boy Prays" from *The Golden Treasury of Prayers for Boys and Girls*. Copyright © 1975 by Western Publishing Company, Inc. Reprinted by permission of the publisher. All rights reserved.

Peek-a-Boo

"Peek-a-boo!
I see you!"
That's baby's favorite rhyme.

"Peek-a-boo!
I see you!"
Time . . .
    after time . . .
        after time.

Teddy Slater

All things bright and beautiful,
　　All creatures great and small,
All things wise and wonderful,
　　The Lord God made them all.

　　Each little flower that opens,
　　Each little bird that sings,
He made their glowing colors,
　　He made their tiny wings.
Cecil Frances Alexander
From "All Things Bright and Beautiful"

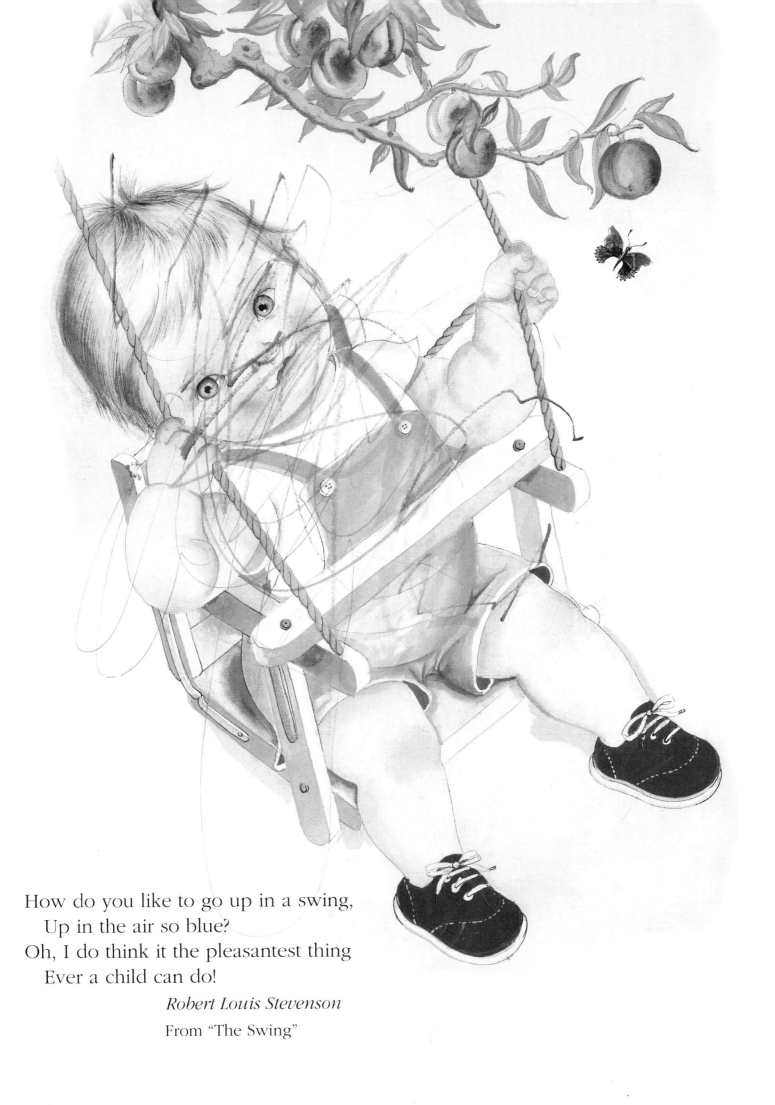

How do you like to go up in a swing,
   Up in the air so blue?
Oh, I do think it the pleasantest thing
   Ever a child can do!

Robert Louis Stevenson

From "The Swing"

The New Baby

Mom says the baby looks like Dad.
Dad says he looks like Mother.
   But I think he
   looks just like me.
What fun to have a brother!

Teddy Slater

My Brother

My brother's worth about two cents,
As far as I can see.
I simply cannot understand
Why they would want a "he."

He spends a good part of his day
Asleep inside the crib,
And when he eats, he has to wear
A stupid baby bib.

He cannot walk and cannot talk
And cannot throw a ball.
In fact, he can't do anything—
He's just no fun at all.

It would have been more sensible,
As far as I can see,
Instead of getting one like him
To get one just like me.

Marci Ridlon

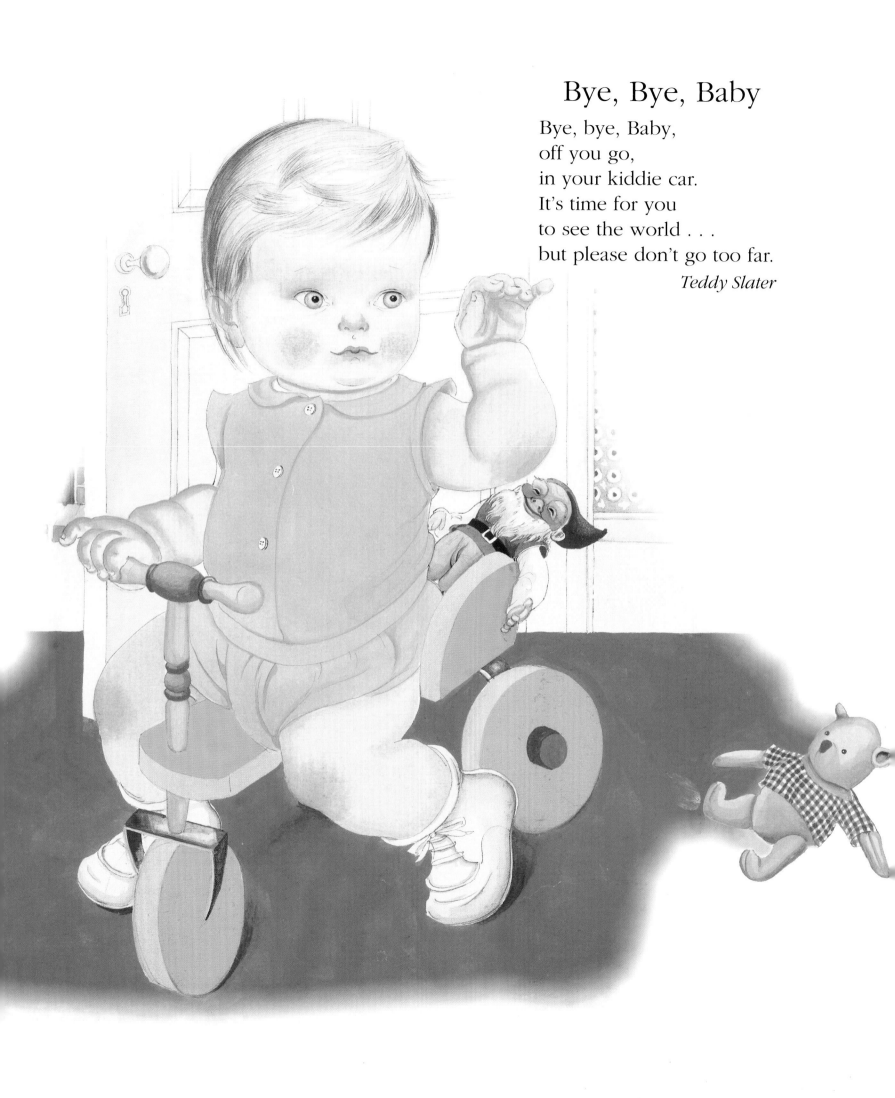

Bye, Bye, Baby

Bye, bye, Baby,
off you go,
in your kiddie car.
It's time for you
to see the world . . .
but please don't go too far.

Teddy Slater

Listen . . .

Floors are creaking, shoes are squeaking,
phones are ringing, Mommy's singing:
    All the sounds that Baby hears
    are music to his ears.

Teddy Slater

The World Is a Rainbow

Brown-eyed baby,
what do you see?
A shiny red apple,
a leafy green tree;
bright yellow birds
in indigo skies:
The world is a rainbow,
made for your eyes.

Teddy Slater

A Kitten's Thought

It's very nice to think of how
In every country lives a Cow
To furnish milk with all her might
For Kitten's comfort and delight.

Oliver Herford

Pussy Willows

Close your eyes
and do not peek
and I'll rub Spring
across your cheek—
smooth as satin,
soft and sleek—
close your eyes
and do not peek.

Aileen Fisher

My Puppy

It's funny
my puppy
knows just how I feel.

When I'm happy
he's yappy
and squirms like an eel.

When I'm grumpy
he's slumpy
and stays at my heel.

It's funny
my puppy
knows such a great deal.
Aileen Fisher

Giant Steps

If I were a giant,
what big steps I'd take.
With one giant step
I'd step over the lake.
With two giant steps
I'd be in the next town
unless I went WHOOPS!
and I fell—
    KA-BOOM
        —down.
Teddy Slater

The Birthday Child

Everything's been different
  All the day long,
Lovely things have happened,
  Nothing has gone wrong.

Nobody has scolded me,
  Everyone has smiled.
Isn't it delicious
  To be a birthday child?

Rose Fyleman

Under

Under the water,
under the sea,
a shimmery
glimmery
world waits for me.

Pink and white coral,
soft silver sand,
the wonder
that's under
I hold in my hand.

Teddy Slater

In meadowlands where creatures stay,
A child sits in quiet play.
She picks the flowers left by rain
And slowly weaves a daisy chain.

Deborah Wilkin Springet
From "The Meadow"

There once was a boy
With a little toy drum—
Rat-a-tat-tat-a-tat
Rum-a-tum-tum.

David Harrison
From "The Boy With a Drum"

Pease Porridge

Pease porridge hot,
Pease porridge cold,
Pease porridge in the pot,
Nine days old.

Some like it hot,
Some like it cold,
Some like it in the pot,
Nine days old.

Mother Goose

Baby's Bath

Gurgle, gurgle, gurgle,
glub-a, glub-a, glub.
What happened to the water
that was in the baby's tub?

Teddy Slater

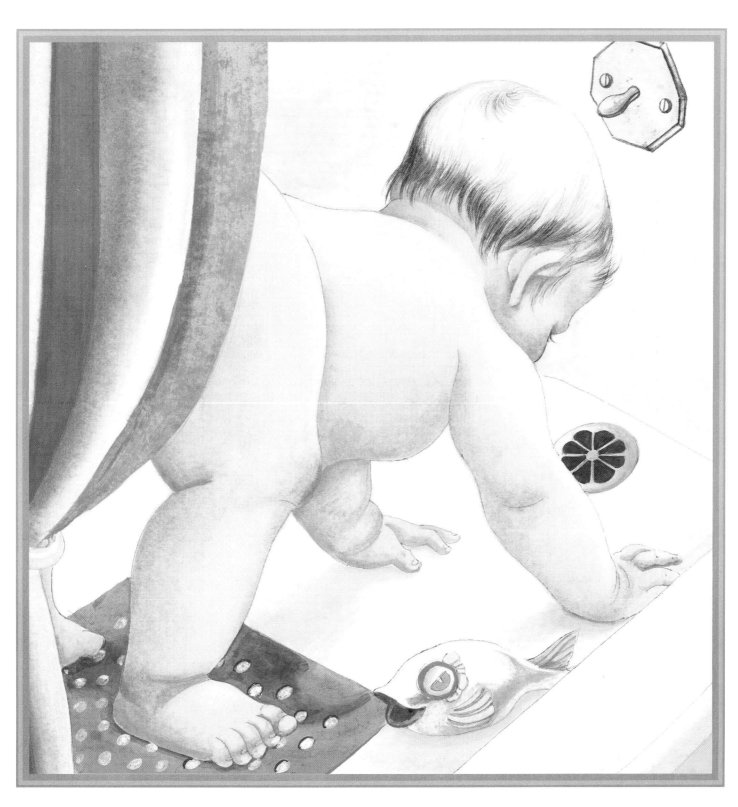

Outside/Inside

Outside the house
   A wild wind is blowing.
   Outside the house
   It's sleeting and snowing.

I'm all bundled up
For this cold winter day,
   But Mommy says I must stay
Inside and play.

           Teddy Slater

I heard the bells on Christmas Day
Their old, familiar carols play,
   And wild and sweet
   The words repeat
Of peace on earth, good-will to men!
      Henry Wadsworth Longfellow
      From "Christmas Bells"

Morning Prayer

Now before we run to play,
let us not forget to pray
to God who kept us through the night
and woke us with the morning light.

Anonymous

A Little Boy Prays

Dear God,
My Mommy is always
    telling me to hurry.
It takes me
    a long time
    to put on my socks,
    she says;
And a long time
    to tie my
    shoelaces.
I tell her
    no matter what
    I'm doing
    I like to
    think about things.
She hugs me
    and calls me
    her little Snail.
He does Your holy
    will slowly,
    she says.
She wants me
    to do Your will, too,
    but a little bit
    faster
    because I'm a boy.
I'll try, dear God. Amen.
Esther Wilkin

I Love Little Pussy

I love little pussy, her coat is so warm,
And if I don't hurt her, she'll do me no harm.
So I'll not pull her tail, nor drive her away,
But pussy and I very gently will play.
I'll sit by the fire, and give her some food,
And pussy will love me, because I am good.

Jane Taylor

Little Boy Blue

Little Boy Blue, come blow your horn!
The sheep's in the meadow,
  the cow's in the corn.
Where is the boy who looks
  after the sheep?
He's under the haystack, fast asleep.
Will you wake him? No, not I;
For if I do, he's sure to cry.

Mother Goose

The year's at the spring
And day's at the morn;
Morning's at seven;
The hillside's dew-pearled;
The lark's on the wing;
The snail's on the thorn;
God's in his heaven—
All's right with the world.

Robert Browning
From "Pippa Passes"

Silly Lily

Lily will not wear her gloves.
She will not wear her sweater.
She won't put on her rubber boots,
no matter what the weather.
But though it may seem very silly,
Lily won't take off her hat.
She just loves her yellow bonnet.
Now what do you think of that?

Teddy Slater

Lullaby

Lullaby, oh lullaby!
Flowers are closed and lambs are sleeping,
   Lullaby, oh lullaby!
Stars are up, the moon is peeping,
   Lullaby, oh lullaby!
While the birds are silence keeping,
   Lullaby, oh lullaby!
Sleep, my baby, fall a-sleeping,
   Lullaby, oh lullaby!

Christina Rossetti